WELCOME TO THE WORLD
OF
Geronimo Stilton

Published by Sweet Cherry Publishing Limited
Unit 36, Vulcan House,
Vulcan Road,
Leicester, LE5 3EF
United Kingdom

First published in the UK in 2020
2020 edition

2 4 6 8 10 9 7 5 3 1

ISBN: 978-1-78226-536-8

Text by Geronimo Stilton
Art Director: Iacopo Bruno
Graphic Designer: Laura Dal Maso / theWorldofDOT
Original cover illustration by Roberto Ronchi (graphics), Manuel A. Puppo and Mirka Andolfo –
Mad 5 (colour)
Internal illustration by Valeria Turati
Artistic Supervisors: Gògo Gò and Certosina Kashmir
Initial and final page illustrations by Roberto Ronchi and Ennio Bufi, MAD5 (design) and Studio
Parlapà and Andrea Cavallini (colour). Map illustrations by Andrea Da Rold and Andrea Cavallini
Cover layout and typography by Margot Reverdiau
Interior layout and typography by Margot Reverdiau
Graphics by Merenguita Gingermouse, Brigitte Torri, Zeppola Zap
© 2004-2015 Edizioni Piemme S.p.A., Palazzo Mondadori – Via Mondadori, 1 – 20090 Segrate
© 2020 UK edition, Sweet Cherry Publishing
International Rights © Atlantyca S.p.A. – via Leopardi 8, 20123 Milano, Italy
Translation © 2007 by Edizioni Piemme S.p.A.

Original title: *La maratona più pazza del mondo*
Based on an original idea by Elisabetta Dami

www.geronimostilton.com/uk

www.sweetcherrypublishing.com

Printed and bound in Turkey
T.IO006

Geronimo Stilton

The Mouse Island MARATHON

Sweet Cherry

HOLEY CHEESE ...

It was a beautiful summer morning. The sun was shining like a round ball of Cheddar in the sky. **What a great day**, I thought as I headed off for work.

Then I missed the bus. I tried running after it, but I had to stop. My heart was **RACING**. My whiskers were sweating. And I could barely breathe!

Holey cheese, I was out of shape! Eventually, I made it to the office. Oops, I almost forgot to introduce myself. My name is Stilton, *Geronimo Stilton*. I am the publisher of The Rodent's Gazette, the most famouse newspaper on Mouse Island.

Anyway, I got to the office just as my sister roared through the lobby. Yes, I mean roared. She likes to ride her motorcycle indoors!

"**WOW**, big brother, I just heard the news. When did you turn into such a sportsmouse?" she chattered, grinning.

I shook my head. I definitely wasn't a *Sportsmouse*. I could barely chew a **cheese stick** and walk at the same time.

Just then, my cousin Trap strolled in. "Hey, **Germeister**. How's the training going? Who would have thought a wimpy rodent like you would become such a sportsmouse?" he snickered.

A minute later, my nephew Benjamin appeared. He tugged at my sleeve. "Uncle **GERONIMO**, what are you doing in the office? A sportsmouse like you should be out running in the park. After all, you're in training," he squeaked.

I twisted my tail up in a knot. Had my whole family gone crazy? The last time I went for a stroll in the park, I tripped over a pine cone and TWISTED my ankle. I was on crutches for **three weeks**!

"Would someone please tell me what you are all SQUEAKING about?" I shouted, plopping down behind my desk.

Before they could answer, a rodent strode into my office. He wore bicycle shorts, sunglasses and a whistle. I would know that mouse anywhere. **It was my friend Champ Strongpaws.**

CHAMP STRONGPAWS

First Name: Champ

Last Name: Strongpaws

Background info: An all-round star athlete. He's into the latest training trends. He works for a sports radio station, and loves to get lazy rodents up and running.

Sports: He does all kinds of endurance sports like cycling, running, and swimming. And he loves marathons!

His advice: Eat right, sleep right, and keep those paws pumping.

What he believes in: Exercise!

His passion: Exploring new countries and getting to experience other cultures.

His slogan: "Sports can make the world a better place!"

His claim to fame: He built a super-fast bicycle that can seat five mice.

His dream: To explore the ten most beautiful countries in the world, in ten days, with ten different bicycles.

A Marathon?

Champ **SLAPPED** me on the back. I checked for broken bones. Did I mention that Champ is a **SUPER-MUSCULAR MOUSE**?

"Oops," he snickered. "Guess I don't know my own strength. Speaking of strength, we'll need to build up those puny muscles of yours, Mr. G. After all, I've entered you in **The Mouse Island Marathon**!"

Marathon? I blinked. I could **NEVER** run a marathon. I couldn't even chew cheese and wiggle my ears at the same time.

But before I could protest, the door to my office burst open. The entire staff of The Rodent's Gazette marched inside. "**Congratulations Geronimo !** You're going to be a **MARATHON** mouse!"

They lifted me up into the air and carried me out of the room. The outer office had been decorated with tonnes of balloons and colourful streamers, and there were **lots of snacks**!

I was just about to stuff my snout with a few yummy doughnuts when Champ slapped them out of my paw.

"None of that, Mr. G," he ordered. "You can't run a marathon unless you eat **HEALTHY** foods."

Then he offered me a carrot stick.

Oh, why did Champ pick me to do something athletic? "So, um, how long is this marathon race thing?" I muttered.

Champ grinned. "It's nothing, Mr. G. Just a mere 26.2 miles."

I almost choked on my carrot. **"Twenty-six miles?!! Twenty-six miles?!!"** I squeaked. "What kind of a race is twenty-six miles long? That's **CRAZY**!"

Champ's grin grew even wider. "That's right, Mr. G. And they call the Mouse Island Marathon the craziest marathon *ever*!"

13

I pictured myself running. But not in the race – away from **Champ Strongpaws**! Far, far away where no one would ever find me. Then I fainted.

Kreamy O'Cheddar, my editor-in-chief, had to revive me with her **Parmesan cheese-scented smelling salts.**

One Two, One Two, One Two ...

The next morning, I was snoring away peacefully in my bed when the doorbell rang.

DING DONG DING DONG

I opened one bleary eye. Who would be ringing my doorbell at such an unmousely hour?

I shuffled to the front door in a daze. Champ was standing on my 'Welcome Rat' mat. "**WAKEY-WAKEY**, Mr. G! Training begins today!" he screeched.

I thought I must be having a **NIGHTMARE**. But then Champ began to sing. Loudly.

"The sun is up, so come on, lazy mousey. Come on out of your cosy housey!"

I put my paws over my ears, hoping Champ would take the hint. **UNFORTUNATELY**, Champ didn't seem to care.

He dragged me out onto my front step in my pyjamas. "Come on, Mr. G, it's time for your morning run." I was **MORTIFIED**. What if someone saw me?

Champ's **squeak** interrupted my thoughts. **"ONE TWO, ONE TWO, KEEP THOSE KNEES UP!"** he yelled. He ran alongside me, checking his stopwatch every few seconds.

I felt sick. My muscles were aching. My head was pounding. Even my fur hurt.

Champ made me run up and down the road thirty times. Finally, I collapsed outside the local flower store. **GREEN PAWS**, the florist, came running out.

"Mr. Stilton, are you feeling **OK**?" he asked worriedly. "You look a little GREEN around the leaves, as we say in the flower business."

I wanted to tell him I was not OK. Far from it. But I was so exhausted, I could hardly breathe. Sweat dripped down my fur like water from a leaky shower.

Two minutes later, I was hit with another shower.

Champ dumped a whole vase of cold water on my head.

"Aaah!" I yelled.

Champ looked satisfied. "Now, **let's see here**, for the rest of the week, your training programme will include a five-mile run, 300 laps in the pool, and two hours of weightlifting. That'll separate the strong mice from the weak, right, Mr. G?" he chuckled.

I wanted to reply, but I was too busy bawling my eyes out.

Oh, how did I get myself into such a mess?

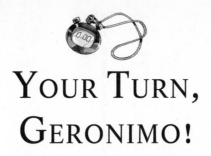

YOUR TURN, GERONIMO!

The next morning, Champ took me to Fastfur Fields, a sports complex for serious athletes. I, **GERONIMO STILTON**, am not a serious athlete.

In the afternoon, Champ took me to play football with some of his friends. I got hit in the head with the ball **twenty-five times!**

Then we were off to Crunchers, New Mouse City's most exclusive gym. Champ made me lift weights. I **fainted**.

Finally, Champ took me to a huge indoor swimming pool. I was doing great until he took my rubber ducky-float away.

The serious sportsmice at Fastfur Fields!

24/7

Days went by. Every morning was the same. Champ woke me up at **6 A.M.** to go running. I started to go to bed in my tracksuit just so I could sleep for a few extra minutes. Did I mention I'm not a morning mouse?

But Champ wouldn't let up. He made me run the same route every day. I ran all over the streets of New Mouse City. I finished at the New Mouse City Public Library. Have you ever been there? You have to climb up sixty-seven steps to even get to the front door.

I didn't climb. I ⟨RAWL⟨D.

Champ ran behind me, shouting advice. "**Don't give up! Don't give in!** Don't give a strange rodent your phone number. It's just not safe," he babbled.

My family loved to watch me run. Trap

waited for me by his kitchen window. He put a piece of cheese on a fishing line and dangled it above my head. "Come and get it, **Gerry Berry**!" he taunted.

Thea chased after me on her motorcycle. "Better move your tail, little brother, or I'll run you over!" she teased.

Then there was Benjamin. Every day he met me at his school bus stop with a delicious yogurt shake. "This is for you, Uncle. You're doing great!" he cheered.

Thank goodness for my **dear sweet nephew**.

After a few weeks, something amazing happened.

I didn't huff and puff when I ran anymore. I didn't feel faint. I didn't cry uncontrollably when I got out of bed in the morning. Well, except for the day I tripped over my catfur rug and broke my pawnail.

Yes, I, **GERONIMO STILTON**, was starting to feel like maybe I wasn't such a sports failure after all.

Of course, working out with Champ wasn't easy. He was in my snout **24/7**. He told me when to run. When to rest. And even what to eat! Champ had thrown out all of the fattening food in my refrigerator, even my **Cheesy Chews**. I was heartbroken. Still, I had to admit I was getting stronger. I had more energy. After three weeks, I even climbed up the steps to the library without stopping!

I surprised everyone, especially myself. **I deserved a reward!** Now if only I could find those **Cheesy Chews** ...

I even climbed up the steps
to the library without stopping!

I Want to Go Hoooome!

Months passed, and Champ made me train harder every day. Soon it was time to set off for the marathon.

The race was going to take place in the city of Nibbles. Nibbles is on the opposite side of Mouse Island, overlooking Stray Cat Harbour.

The plane ride took twenty million hours. Well, OK, maybe not twenty million, but it was **SUPER-LONG**.

I tried to take a nap, but Champ wanted to give me advice about the marathon. "Now listen up, Mr. G. Whatever you do, don't worry about the twenty-six long, exhausting, painful, back-breaking miles ahead of you. Don't worry if you're moving **slower** than a snail with arthritis. Don't worry if you feel *weaker* than an ant with a broken leg. Don't worry if you're more **TIRED** than a hibernating sloth. Just concentrate on finishing the race," he squeaked.

Oh, why had I agreed to enter this crazy race? I wasn't an athlete. I was a newspaper mouse. **"I want to go home!"** I sobbed.

But Champ just grinned. "Don't be **ridiculous**, Mr. G. I didn't spend all that time training you for nothing. You'll do great."

To take my mind off things, I decided to read the paper. Bad idea. Staring up at me from the front page was a photo of a **HUGE, TERRIFYING CAT**. Felinius ferociousmus, otherwise known as Fifi the cat, was an extremely rare species. She had escaped from the Natural Science Mouseum of Nibbles, where scientists had been studying her. Now the whole city of Nibbles was running from Fifi.

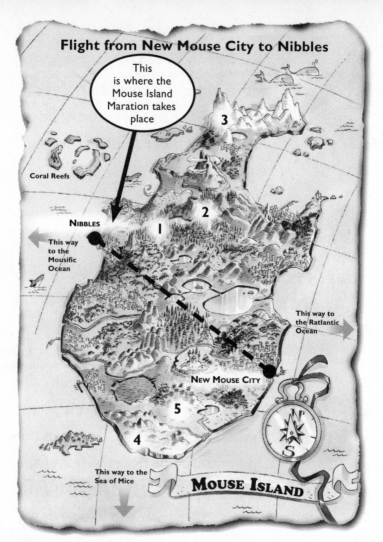

Flight from New Mouse City to Nibbles

This is where the Mouse Island Maration takes place

Coral Reefs

NIBBLES

This way to the Mousific Ocean

This way to the Ratlantic Ocean

NEW MOUSE CITY

This way to the Sea of Mice

MOUSE ISLAND

1. Brimstones Lake
2. Roastedrat Volcano
3. Frozen Fur Park
4. Mousehara Desert
5. Rio Mosquito

The City of Nibbles is on the westernmost tip of Mouse Island. It overlooks the Rattenburg River and Stray Cat Harbour, famous for its huge (and very hungry) sharks.

Nibbles is known for its very strange climate, which is constantly changing. When the north wind blows, the temperatures are icy and when the south wind blows it's like living in an oven!

THE CITY OF NIBBLES

Route of the Mouse Island Marathon

I stared at the picture of the horrifying wild cat. Then I noticed my fellow passengers. They looked as **WILD** as Fifi. And they were all headed to the marathon, too.

How did I know they were marathon runners? That's easy:

1. They were *all* wearing expensive tracksuits.

2. They *all* took turns racing one another **up** and **down** the aisles.

3. They *all* drank from **big** water bottles.

4. They *all* ate energy bars.

5. They *all* read fitness magazines.

6. They *all* had *BIG* muscles.

7. They *all* looked like they'd be finished with the race before I even crossed the starting line!

I sank down in my seat. Oh, when would this **NIGHTMARE** be over?

Finally, it was time for lunch. At last, something to celebrate! I licked my whiskers. Right then, the flight attendant passed me a plate. **Three lettuce leaves**, **TWO RAW CARROTS** and a boiled turnip stared back at me.

I pulled the attendant aside. "Um, excuse me, madam. Is there any way you could get me something a little less healthy? Like a big slab of Cheddar lasagne?" I whispered.

The flight attendant smiled. But next to me, Champ frowned. **RATS!**

"Mr. G, I'm very disappointed in you," he scolded. "You know you're in training. In fact, madam, can you please remove one of these lettuce leaves? My friend here is on a very strict diet."

I chewed my pawnail in dismay. Oh, if only it were a delicious piece of chocolate cake!

With a sigh, I picked up a carrot. I took a bite. It tasted like a piece of rubber. **YUCK!**

After the carrot, I needed to get rid of the rubber taste. I picked up my cup. It was filled with some kind of **STRANGE, LUMPY BROWN LIQUID**. I think it was one of those energy drinks. I took a sip. I gagged. This drink sure gave me energy. I felt like hurling my cup out the window!

I picked up a carrot.

I was so **hungry**, I decided there was only one thing left to do. I had to use my imagination. I pretended the carrot was a slice of cheese pizza and the

I picked up my cup.

36

I tried gulping them down together

energy drink was a **YUMMY MOZZARELLA MILKSHAKE**. Quickly, I tried gulping them down together. It didn't work. **All I tasted was rubber and a cross between sour gherkins and curdled milk.**

All I tasted was rubber and curdled milk.

DIIIIIING! DIIIIIING!

At last, the plane landed in Nibbles.

I was exhausted. When we reached the hotel, I crawled straight into bed.

"Don't forget to set your alarm clock. The big race is tomorrow," Champ reminded me.

I sat up in bed. **HOLEY CHEESE!** I was so tired, I had forgotten all about the marathon. I started to worry. What if I tripped? What if I fainted?

I didn't shut my eyes until 6 a.m. Two minutes later, the alarm went off.

Diiiiing! Diiiiing!

I WAS A WRECK.

When I got to the hotel lobby, I noticed something strange. A lot of the other runners had bags under their eyes, too.

Maybe I wasn't the only one who was nervous!

A mouse with pretty honey-coloured fur tapped my shoulder.

"Is this your first marathon?" she asked. "Mine, too. I'm Honey Fur."

I smiled. Maybe this marathon business wasn't so bad after all.

"Um, yes, well, uh, my name is Stilton, *Geronimo Stilton* ..." I began.

But I was interrupted by Champ. He stood on a

THE MARATHON

The oldest long-distance running race became an Olympic sport at the world's first modern edition of the games in 1896.

The name marathon goes back to 490 B.C. when the Greek soldier Pheidippides ran from the battlefield of Marathon to Athens (24.85 miles) to announce victory over the Persians.

The length of the marathon was initially fixed according to the distance run by Pheidippides (24.85 miles), but following the 1908 London Olympics, the distance was changed to its present length: 26.2 miles. This corresponds to the distance between Windsor Castle (where the race began) and the White City stadium (where it ended).

Over the years, the marathon has been adopted as a major sporting event by several of the world's most important cities. The oldest annual marathon is the Boston Marathon, which has been around since 1897!

platform near a huge open window. In one paw he held a microphone. In the other he held a stack of notecards.

"Dear rodent friends, I'd like to welcome you all to **The Mouse Island Marathon**," he squeaked, reading his speech off the cards.

"For some of you, this is your **FIRST** marathon, and I want to congratulate you on your courage. You will soon see that running a marathon is a truly wonderful experience."

Right then, a big gust of wind blew in the window. It picked up Champ's cards and tossed them all over the room.

"My speech," Champ muttered, looking lost. I decided to help Champ out. I grabbed the microphone from him.

"Um, well, hello, my name is **GERONIMO STILTON**, and I'm very excited to be running my first marathon today," I stammered. "I've been training really hard for this race. I've even given up all of my favourite foods, like **TRIPLE DELUXE CHEDDAR BURGERS** and my dear aunt RATILDA's homemade cream cheese."

Before I knew it, I was drooling all over the microphone.

I looked around. The other runners were drooling too. Champ glared at me. Uh-oh.

I didn't mean to cause a scene, making everyone remember the foods they'd given up. **Still, could I help it if I just couldn't say no to cream cheese?**

IT FIGURES ...

Before I knew it, it was time to start the race. Runners spilled out of the hotel. We were greeted by a rush of frozen air. It was **SNOWING!**

Luckily, I was prepared. I pulled a hat over my ears and wrapped a scarf around my snout. I stumbled blindly through the snow. A minute later, I walked **SMACK** into another runner. "Watch where you're going, Furball," the mouse muttered. His voice sounded familiar. It was **Gloomy Gus von Cacklefur**! He was the uncle of my strange friend, *Creepella von Cacklefur*. Gloomy Gus was just as weird as his niece. And he was always complaining about something.

"It figures we'd get stuck running in the middle of a snowstorm, eh, Geronimo?" he grumbled. "The weather in Nibbles is the worst. When the north wind blows, your fur turns to icicles. When the south wind blows, you can fry an egg on your snout."

I listened politely as Gloomy Gus moaned and groaned about, well, everything. I shook my head in sympathy. What else could I do? There was no cheering up old Gloomy Gus. **In fact, if you looked up the word miserable in the dictionary, you'd probably find his picture next to it.**

KEEP YOUR PAWS ON THE GROUND!

The marathon's starting line was on a giant bridge. I could hardly believe the crowd. It was **huge**! There were young rodents, old rodents, and rodents of all different sizes, shapes, and colours. There were serious athletes and **CHEESE PUFFS**, like me.

Some athletes were blind and were paired with guides. Others were in special wheelchairs, which they moved using their paws.

It was *AMAZING*! Suddenly, I began to get excited. "Yes, Geronimo!" I told myself. "You can do it."

Then, out of the corner of my

eye, I spotted a beat-up old pickup truck. The rat who was driving it looked just like an undertaker. A sign on the back of the truck read, 'REST IN PIECES'.

"Don't worry if you don't make it. I'll pick up your remains," the rat snickered through the window.

A shiver ran down my fur. Oh, who was I kidding? I wasn't an athlete. I couldn't run a marathon. Even though it was **FREEZING** outside, I broke into a sweat. My head began to **POUND**. My paws shook.

An old mouse patted me on the shoulder.

"Don't be nervous, Sonny. All you have to do is keep your paws on the ground and keep reaching for the stars," he advised. "My name is **OLD RAT RICKETY**, but you can call me Rickety for short. I've been running marathons for thirty-five years, and let me tell you, they never get boring. Yep, something tells me this one's going to be the craziest one yet!"

I gulped. **OLD RAT RICKETY** was starting to look a little crazy himself. His eyes gleamed. His whiskers whirled in the wind. Before he moved on, he whispered one last bit of advice in my ear.

"Just remember, Sonny," he squeaked. "**Never give up**. Never stop believing in yourself. And never get the prune cheese rolls at Stop and Squeak. **THEY'RE AWFUL!**"

OLD RAT RICKETY

I was about to ask Rickety what he thought about the cherry cheese Danish, when a mouse wearing an official-looking suit held up his paw.

Everyone on the bridge grew silent.

"ALL MARATHON RUNNERS LINE UP, PLEASE!" the mouse squeaked into a megaphone.

Then he blew a horn so loud I nearly jumped right out of my fur. **The marathon was starting!**

On Your Marks, Get Set ... Go!

"On your marks, get set ... go!!!" the official mouse yelled.

And we were off. I must admit, it was incredible. Thirty-two thousand rodents running all at once!

I took off along the bridge.

After a little while, we hit a sign that read '**Mile One**'. I was so **PROUD** of myself. So far, I didn't feel tired at all.

I guess all those torturous mornings with Champ had really paid off.

On both sides of the road, the crowd cheered us along.

"BRAVO, BRAVO!" an old mouse with white fur cried.

"You can do it!" his friend added.

"Yippee!" A baby mouselet clapped her paws.

Everyone wanted to see us run. I felt like a real

celebrity. I pushed my shoulders back and straightened my scarf, just in case anyone wanted to take my picture. You never know.

Some of the spectators carried signs. They said things like, **'KEEP UP THE PACE!'**, **'YOU'RE THE BEST!'** and **'Shake a paw, Grandma Beady Eyes!'**

That last one gave me a **tiny** pang. I wished my

family could have been there to cheer me on, too.

After three miles, I stopped at a water station. Champ always told me how important it is to drink liquids while you're exercising.

A smiling race assistant passed me a plastic cup of water. Then he threw his paws around my neck. At first, I panicked. Was he trying to strangle me? **WAS HE AFTER MY EXPENSIVE CHEDDAR-COLOURED SCARF?**

Then the mouse squeaked in my ear, **"Surprise, Uncle!"** It was my nephew Benjamin. "I'm here to cheer you on. You're doing great!" he cried.

Did I mention I have the sweetest nephew in the world?

SNAP OUT OF IT!

After seeing Benjamin, I had new energy. I ran and ran.

I was actually feeling OK. But after thirteen miles, everything started to go downhill. No, I'm not talking about the road. I'm talking about yours truly. I felt **AWFUL**!

My paws were heavier than two blocks of my grouchy grandma Onewhisker's fruit cheesecakes. My knees were **SHAKING**. And I had **SPRAINED** my tail.

I wanted to stop. I wanted to rest. I wanted to check into the nearest day spa and get a two-hour massage.

Just then, the **creepy** rat with the beat-up pickup truck pulled alongside me. He opened the door.

"Ready to give up? I'll take you away," he smirked.

I was so scared that I took off again, sobbing like a newborn mouselet.

"I CAN'T DO IT! I CAN'T DO IT!" I wailed.

"**Snap out of it, little brother.** Of course you can do it!" a familiar voice called out.

I stopped crying and opened my eyes wide. Trap and Thea were standing right in front of me.

In a flash, Trap shoved a thick piece of cheddar into my mouth. "The mouse in the cheese store told me this cheddar has double the protein of your ordinary cheese. You'd better like it, **Germeister**. It cost me a bundle," he squeaked.

I gobbled down the cheese in one bite. It was
AMAZING.

But I still wanted to quit.

"This marathon is **too long** for me ..."
I blubbered.

Thea rolled her eyes. "Of course it's
long," she snickered. "That's why it's
called a marathon. Now stop WHINING
and **start running**. You don't want to
tell Champ he wasted his time with you,
do you?"

I gulped. Thea was right. Champ would have a fit if
I gave up now.

I kept on running. **Oh, my aching paws!**

55

Roasted Mouse!

After twenty miles, the south wind started blowing. It came from the Mousehara Desert. Now it was **HOT**, **HOT, HOT!**

I took off my hat, scarf, and tracksuit. It was **BOILING!** My whiskers were dripping with sweat.

At that moment, the sky turned a funny yellow colour. Before I could say cheese niblets, there was a tremendous blast of wind. A second later, I couldn't see a thing! I was covered from head to paw with sand. It was a **SANDSTORM!**

"Everyone get down!" another runner yelled. We crouched down together behind a wall. It sheltered us from the wind and sand. We covered our snouts with handkerchiefs, so that the sand couldn't get in our mouths and noses.

A car motor rumbled in the distance. I just knew it

was that creepy rat in the pickup truck. He couldn't wait for someone to drop.

I shivered. I hoped it wouldn't be me.

I decided to pass the time by humming nursery rhymes. Everyone joined in. We were just finishing the second chorus of 'Pop Goes the Gerbil', when the storm ended.

I wiped off my glasses, said goodbye to the other runners, and took off.

Bzzzz ... Bzzzz ... Bzzzz!

I had only gone a little farther when I heard a strange buzzing noise.

The buzzing got **louder** and **louder**.

All of a sudden, a black cloud fell over me. It was a giant swarm of bloodthirsty *MOSQUITOES*!

The mosquitoes made a feast of my fur. I felt like the strawberry cheesecake at my nephew's birthday party. Every bug wanted a piece of me!

I tried slapping them away, but it was no use. They just kept coming back for more. I was being *eaten alive*! Headlines flashed before my eyes:

MOUSE-HUNGRY MOSQUITOES MAKE A MEAL OUT OF PUBLISHER! GERONIMO STILTON: ALL CHEWED UP AND NOWHERE TO GO!

Finally, after I ran and ran, the buzzing stopped. I opened one eye. **The cloud of black mosquitoes swirled off into the sky.**

WET UP TO THE WHISKERS!

I was so happy to be away from the sand and the mosquitoes. For a moment, I almost forgot that I was running in a crazy marathon. I felt the warm sun on my fur. I listened to the birds singing in the trees. *Ah, what a beautiful day,* I thought.

Then I noticed a **PRETTY** little pond off to the side of the road. It looked so calm and peaceful. I scampered over and dipped one sore paw into the water. The cold water felt fabumouse! I leaned over to splash my snout. Big mistake.

SPLASH!

I fell headfirst into the pond. I was WET UP to MY WHISKERS! Green scum from the bottom of the pond stuck to my fur as I pulled myself out of the water.

Just then, the rat in the pickup truck pulled up.

"You smell worse than the mice at the morgue," he snickered. "Ready to call it quits? I'm sure they'd love to meet you."

I shivered. Pond scum flew in all directions.

SMACK!

Some of it hit the driver right in the snout. He took off with a scowl.

"That'll teach him," I giggled to myself.

A School in Flames

I started running again. My paws **POUNDED** the pavement. Just as I turned the corner, it smelled like something was burning. In the distance, I could see a school building sitting on a hill.

FLAMES SHOT FROM THE ROOF!

I signalled to some of the other runners. "Quick, they need our help!" I squeaked.

We got there in the nick of time. Crying mouselets stumbled out of the exits, while their teachers tried to keep them calm.

One mouselet was **missing**.

I didn't stop. I just ran inside. **BURNING** embers were falling everywhere. The roof started to cave in.

I was **SCARED** out of my fur. But what could I do? I had to find that mouselet.

Finally, I found the terrified mouse in the school's

music room. He was hiding under the piano. I scooped him up and carried him outside to safety.

Everyone clapped and cheered when we emerged safely outside. I felt like a **BIG CHEESE**.

I took off on the race again. **But this time, I had a huge smile on my snout.**

EARTHQUAKE!

I was still smiling as I scampered by a grassy field. But before long, I noticed something **ODD**. The grass seemed to be rising.

I squinted. What was going on? Was I dreaming? Was I going blind? Was I headed for the Mad Mouse Centre?

Just then, the earth began to **SHAKE** beneath my paws. Now I knew what was going on. I had read about it in The City of Nibbles Guidebook. Every ten years or so, the place got hit by an earthquake.

RAT-MUNCHING RATTLESNAKES!

I felt faint with fear. I took off my glasses so I could cry freely. **"I WANT MY MUMMY!"** I squeaked. Then I noticed a blurry figure to one side of me. I squinted. It was Honey Fur, the pretty rodent I had met at the beginning of the race. Oh, why did I always have to act like such a 'fraidy mouse?

Just then, we heard someone shouting. A gaping chasm had opened up in the middle of the road. One of the runners was about to **FALL** to the bottom.

I had an idea. Quickly, I gathered everyone's running jackets. I tied them together to form a rope. Then we pulled the runner to safety.

Honey Fur patted my paw. "Great idea," she whispered.

I grinned. Score one for the 'fraidy mouse!

HOLD ON TIGHT!

I was so proud of myself. I felt a sudden burst of energy. I felt strong. I felt focused. I felt … **WET**! I looked down. **HOLEY CHEESECAKE!** I was so busy rescuing the other runner, I hadn't heard the sound of rushing water.

"**LOOK OUT!** The Rattenburg River has burst

its banks!" a mouse called.

All of the marathoners began to panic. Crashing waves suddenly surrounded us. I was **TERRIFIED**. I grabbed the paw of the mouse next to me. That gave me an idea.

"**Hold on tight to each other.** If we do that, maybe we won't be swept away!" I yelled.

We formed a marathon mouse chain. **It worked!** We didn't get carried away by the river. Slowly, the waves subsided.

We were ready to race again!

GREAT-GRANDMOTHER STINKYFUR

I was about to take off when I saw a runner by the side of the road. She was staring sadly at the ground. Tears trickled down her fur.

"Are you OK?" I asked.

The rodent wrung her paws. "I've lost my watch. It means so much to me. It belonged to my **great-grandmother Stinkyfur**. Oh, I just have to find it," she sobbed.

I felt sorry for her. I felt sorry for Great-Grandmother Stinkyfur, too. I mean, did her fur actually **STINK**? I figured now wasn't the time to ask.

Instead, I searched the ground for the lost watch.

Time passed. The other runners were long gone.

"I don't want to keep you, **MR. STILTON**," the mouse said, sighing. "Please go back and finish the race."

At that very moment, I thought I saw something shining in the dust. I bent down. Could it be? It was!

"MY WATCH!" the mouse squeaked. **She threw her paws around me in a bone-crushing hug.**

CHEESEBALLS IN THE ROAD?

I took a deep breath and rejoined the race. I was feeling pretty strong. I could hardly believe it. I was doing it!

Two seconds later, the muscular rodent in front of me fell to the ground. What was it this time? Cheeseballs in the road?

I looked around. Nothing seemed unusual.

"Are you OK?" I asked the muscular rodent. By now, he was rolling around on the ground, clutching his tummy.

"Oh, I am such a fool!", the mouse cried. "I stopped at that Spicy Rat stand on the side of the road. Now I have an **AWFUL STOMACH ACHE**."

I nodded sympathetically. I mean, who can resist a piping-**HOT** Cheddar burrito? Yummy!

"Ahem, well, maybe I can help," I offered. "I have

a weak stomach, too." I pulled a **SWISS CHEESE-FLAVOURED** mint from my pocket. "Here, try this," I squeaked.

The big mouse sat down on the curb and popped the mint in his mouth. A few minutes later, he jumped up.

"**GERONIMO**, you're my **hero**! I feel like a new mouse!" he squeaked. Then he smacked me on the back in thanks and took off.

Forget Bigpaws, that mouse should change his name to Gigundo Paws!

I LOST MY MUMMY!

I was still checking for broken bones when I heard a mouse crying. What now? Had someone twisted a tail? Lost a lottery ticket? Forgotten to cross **at the green** and not in between? Then I spotted a very small mouse crying behind a bush.

"I LOST MY MUMMY!" he wailed.

I had to stop. What could I do? After all, I am a gentlemouse. I picked up the tyke and dried his tears.

"My name is **GERONIMO STILTON**," I told him. "Why don't we go find a nice policemouse? He'll be able to help us look for your mummy."

The little mouse smiled. Then he blew his nose on my top. Oh, the price of being a gentlemouse.

I led the little mouse to the police station. Within a few minutes, a female mouse came rushing in. **"PIPSQUEAK!"** she cried. "I was worried sick about you! My glasses fell off, and I couldn't find you in the crowd." She picked up her son and hugged him tight.

Then she hugged me. Then a policemouse. Then a chair, a desk, and a filing cabinet before she headed out the door.

I grinned and set off on the race again.

THE PRETTIEST BLUE EYES

I was just starting to pick up the pace again when the mouse next to me tripped.

"**OUCH!**" she cried, rubbing her paw. Her name was **Sugarsnout Snap**, and she had the prettiest blue eyes I had ever seen.

"I think I sprained my paw! I guess I'm out of the race," Sugarsnout said, sighing.

I felt **AWFUL**. I just had to do something. "Let's go to the first aid station. I'm sure they'll be able to help you," I suggested.

Sugarsnout leaned on my shoulder, and off we went.

It took us a while to get the first aid station. It must have been **TWO THOUSAND MILES AWAY**. Well, OK, maybe not two thousand, but you get the picture. **It took us forever!**

Lucky for me, Sugarsnout was **great** company. We talked about books and food. Two of my favourite topics! Yep, that Sugarsnout was a mouse after my own heart.

When we reached the first aid station, I was having so much fun I DIDN'T WANT TO LEAVE. But Sugarsnout told me to go on ahead. She'd meet me at the finish line.

Now I had another reason to make it to the end!

JUST LIKE
SUPERMOUSE!

I SCAMPERED OFF AGAIN. As I passed the twenty-third mile marker, I saw a mouse who looked just like my dear **Aunt Sweetfur**.

"That's it, young mouse! **You can do it!**" she shouted encouragingly.

I smiled and waved. That's when I noticed *a shifty-looking rodent*. He was standing right next to the **Aunt Sweetfur** lookalike. In a *FLASH*, he grabbed her handbag and **took off into the crowd**.

I had to do something! I ran after the thief. My heart pounded with fear. What if he had a weapon, like a can of rodent spray? Was I ready to go paws-up for a handbag?

I glanced back at the little old lady mouse. She was sobbing into her little-old-lady-mouse handkerchief. I felt a **SURGE OF ENERGY**. With one final lunge, I grabbed the thief's tail. I ripped the bag out of his paws and returned it to the old lady.

"You were just like SUPERMOUSE," she sighed.

I wished it were true. I was feeling more like **Totally Exhausted Mouse**.

THE BRIDGE OF SQUEAKS

I stumbled back into the race. At last, I reached an **ENORMOUSE** bridge. I remembered Champ had told me this was called the Bridge of Squeaks. Now I knew why. It was at such a steep angle, it took **every last squeak** to make it across!

All of the runners around me were groaning. I heard one cry, **"THAT'S IT! I'M DONE!"**

Another sobbed, "I've got too many blisters! I'll never make it to the end!"

"This is crazy!" a third wailed.

I felt the same way. What kind of a **NUTTY** mouse wants to run a marathon, anyway?

Just then, I spotted **OLD RAT RICKETY** running nearby. He had a **HUGE SMILE** on his face. Speaking of **NUTTY**! Then I remembered the old rat's words of advice: *Never give up. Never stop believing in yourself.*

I took a deep breath. If **OLᴅ RAT RICKETY** could do it, so could I. I scampered forward with every last bit of strength in my paws.

I was **almost** to the top of the bridge when a **TERRIBLE** thing happened. A runner fainted and fell into the water below!

What could I do? I had to help.

Before I could talk myself out of it, **I DIVED IN AFTER HIM**.

The water was colder than the super-chilly deep freeze slushy at The Icy Rat ice cream parlour. Even my whiskers were **FROZEN**. But I didn't have time to think about that. I searched **FRANTICALLY** for the runner. Then I saw him sinking below the surface of the water nearby.

CHEESE NIBLETS! He looked just like, well, a drowning rat! There was no time to lose. I dived down under the water and grabbed him by the tail. Then I swam to the surface.

Suddenly, I heard a roaring sound above me. I looked up and saw a **HELICOPTER**. It was coming to rescue us.

"Here! We're over here!" I shouted, waving my paw in the air.

The helicopter lowered a long metal cable with a life ring attached to the end of it.

Once I grabbed onto the life ring, the rescue workers pulled me and the other runner up together.

They wrapped us in warm blankets. The doctor checked us out. **I was fine**, but the runner I had saved needed to rest overnight in a hospital. They delivered him to a waiting ambulance.

"Now where can we drop you, **MR. STILTON**?" the helicopter pilot asked me. Lots of places came to

mind, like a gourmet cheese store or a tropical island. But a little voice inside my head kept nagging me. It said, *NEVER GIVE UP! NEVER GIVE UP!*

What could I do? I had to go on with the marathon. That voice was giving me a **mouse-sized headache!** I asked the pilot to drop me off at the exact place on the bridge where I had stopped running.

PEE-YEW!

I caught up with some of the other marathoners. We ran across the bridge and through the city streets. We passed by a fish market. Pee-yew, it stunk! I tried holding my snout and running, but I kept tripping over my paws. Did I mention I'm not the most coordinated mouse on the block?

Just then, I heard a sound behind me. A sardine truck had jumped the kerb. Fish spilled out all over the street! The driver stood nearby, wringing his paws. **"NOW WHAT AM I GOING TO DO?"** he moaned. "I have to deliver these fish today."

I felt sorry for him. What if he had been delivering The Rodent's Gazette? I would want someone to help him. I had to do something, even if the fish were stinky. I organised the other runners to help with the clean-up.

When we were finished, the truck driver gave me a hug. It felt nice to do another good deed. Well, except for the **STINKY, SLIMY, FISHY PART**.

I waved goodbye to the truck driver and took off running again. As I ran, I peeked at my watch. **HOLEY CHEESE!** It was late. I didn't have far to go, but at this rate, I'd be running into the night. **Yikes! Did I mention I'm afraid of the dark?**

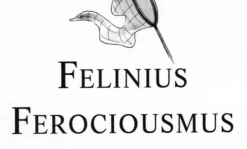

FELINIUS
FEROCIOUSMUS

I was still thinking about running in the dark when I heard a sound. A STRANGE sound.

Well, actually, it was more of a **TERRIFYING** sound. it sounded like the meowing of a **HUNGRY CAT**! But what would a cat be doing at a marathon for mice? I gulped. Something told me it wouldn't be part of the cheering section.

With a squeak, I forced myself to turn around. **BIG MISTAKE.**

I found myself snout-to-snout with a **MASSIVE BEAST**. It had snow-coloured fur, blazing yellow eyes and razor-sharp fangs. Its claws were so huge, they looked like kitchen knives!

I almost **fainted**. It was the huge, hairy feline I had seen in the paper! Yep, the one that had escaped

from the Natural Science Mouseum of Nibbles. Felinius ferociousmus, otherwise known as Fifi, stared at me with evil, hungry eyes. This was it. **I WAS A DEAD MOUSE.** "Goodbye, cruel mouse world!" I sobbed as I turned and raced through the streets.

Behind me, I could hear Fifi licking her chops. My aches and pains disappeared. My paws felt as light as feathers. It's amazing what being chased by a cat can do to a mouse. I felt like an Olympic athlete!

"Make way! Make way!" I shouted as I ran.

The other runners jumped aside. I guess no one wanted to be Fifi's dinner. But me? I kept going at **SUPERSONIC SPEED** for what seemed like forever.

I was so worried about Fifi, **I didn't even realise I had reached the finish line**. I ran right through the tape and kept on going.

Then I spotted the mouseum workers making their way through the crowd. In an amazing manoeuvre, they captured Fifi in an **enormouse** net and took her away.

I collapsed in a heap. "I'm alive!" I squeaked weakly. Then I fainted.

My dear nephew Benjamin was standing over me when I woke up. "Uncle, I knew you were good, but I never imagined that you would come in $FIRST$!" he shrieked.

"F-FIRST?" I spluttered.

At that moment, the crowd lifted me up and tossed me high into the air.

"Hooray for Geronimo Stilton!" they cheered. "The winner of the Mouse Island Marathon!"

Tears sprang to my eyes. I felt so **HAPPY**. So **proud**. So dizzy. **Did I mention I'm afraid of heights?**

NEVER GIVE UP!

Old Rat Rickety shook my paw. "Well done, Sonny!" he squeaked. "I'm so glad you took my advice. **Never give up. Never stop believing in yourself.** And never get your tail stuck in a revolving door. Let me tell you, that hurts!"

I was about to ask **RICKETY** more about the door incident, when the national anthem of Mouse Island began to play. I was so humbled. **They were playing it in my honour!**

After the national anthem, there was a fancy awards ceremony. Everyone was there: my family, **OLD RAT RICKETY**, **HONEY FUR**, even **Sugarsnout**. I got to stand on the block with the number one on it. Then an official-looking mouse put a shiny medal around my neck. **I COULD HARDLY BELIEVE IT.** I felt like

I was in the middle of a crazy DREAM. I mean, how else could I have come in **FIRST** place? I was the least athletic mouse around. I couldn't lift a half-kilo weight. I couldn't use a skipping rope. And I was always the last rodent picked for the team.

Just then, I spotted Champ in the crowd. "I'd like to thank my family, and especially my friend and trainer Champ Strongpaws for entering me in this marathon," I squeaked. I watched as a tear slid down his snout. I was glad I had made him proud. Maybe now he'd finally tell me where he'd hidden my precious **Cheesy Chews**.

NATIONAL ANTHEM OF MOUSE ISLAND

A thousand tails
raised in the air.
A thousand voices
squeak with care.
Rodents cheer and
heave a sigh.
Sweet Mouse Island
will never die!

MARATHON IN THE RATTYTRAP JUNGLE?

A few hours later, we boarded the plane back to New Mouse City. Ah, it felt good to go home. I was so **TIRED**. I couldn't wait to kick up my paws and **relax**!

That night, I treated myself to a delicious cheesy lasagne dinner. Then I crawled into bed and fell fast asleep. I dreamed I was holidaying at a peaceful island resort.

The next morning, I went into the office early. I had decided that my dream must have been a sign. Yep, I was in desperate need of a little R&R. I would take the rest of the week off and relax at my favourite resort and spa, **THE RESTFUL RODENT**. But first, I needed to tell my staff.

"Excuse me, I have an announcement

to make. I am going to be taking a week off ..." I began.

At that moment, a very muscular rodent burst into the office. Can you guess who it was? Yes, it was Champ Strongpaws.

"Mr. G, you must have a sixth sense!" he cried. "How did you know I just signed you up for another marathon?"

I blinked. **"Another m-m-m-marathon?"** I stammered.

Champ's grin lit up the room. "That's right, Mr. G. You'll be taking part in the Rattytrap Jungle Marathon on the Rio Mosquito. Isn't that great?" he cried.

I felt faint. "This isn't happening," I told myself. The Rattytrap Jungle was the **SCARIEST** place in the world. I knew, because I'd been there on one of my previous adventures. It was filled with poisonous snakes, raging rivers and deadly spiders.

No way was I going back there.

But how was I going to tell Champ?

I decided honesty was the best policy. After all, that's what my dear **Aunt Sweetfur** always told me. So

I calmly explained to Champ that I'm not really much of a sportsmouse. I like working in my office. I like reading books. I like relaxing in my mouse hole.

Champ just yawned. **"Boring!"** he snickered. Then he waved an airline ticket under my snout. "Besides, it's too late to back out now. We're leaving in an hour. The marathon is tomorrow!"

My jaw hit the ground. **"TOMORROW?"** I squeaked.

At that moment, my favourite nephew Benjamin popped into the room.

"Uncle Geronimo, I hear you're going to be in another marathon. Can I come with you? Please? Please? I always knew you were like **Supermouse**," he said.

I agreed. What else could I do? I knew I wasn't like Supermouse, but **I really did have a super nephew.**

ALL IN ONE DAY

HOW DID IT GO?

Well, let's just say the jungle is a very, very dangerous place. I was chased by a snapping crocodile, hunted down by a ferocious tiger, and practically strangled by a giant mouse-eating snake. **MOULDY MOZZARELLA!**

Yes, you might even say it was crazier than the Mouse Island Marathon. Still, I would always remember my experience in Nibbles. After all, not every mouse gets to run a marathon, nab a thief, save a drowning rodent, survive an earthquake, and **catch an escaped Felinius ferociousmus all in one day, right?**

CHAMP'S

TOP TEN TIPS

FOR BECOMING A

SUPERMOUSE!

1. Eat the right foods!

Start the day with a good breakfast: it'll give you energy! Try not to eat too many crisps, fried foods, sweets, chocolate, or desserts, when possible. They are difficult to digest and usually don't have the nutrients your body really needs!

Try these, instead. These nutrients will give you lots of energy for exercising.

It's OK to eat all different kinds of food ... but in the right quantities. Not too much, and not too little! To stay healthy, it's important to eat healthy foods and get plenty of exercise.

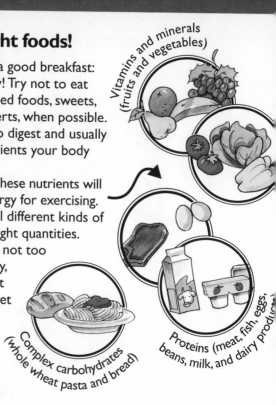

Vitamins and minerals (fruits and vegetables)

Proteins (meat, fish, eggs, beans, milk, and dairy products)

Complex carbohydrates (whole wheat pasta and bread)

2. Drink at least eight glasses of water a day!

Water is a very important part of staying healthy. Eight glasses is a good daily amount.

When you play sports or when it's very hot, you have to drink even more water. Otherwise, you could become dehydrated. Dehydration occurs when you lose more liquids than you actually drink.

Try not to drink too many fizzy drinks, like cola, because they make your tummy swell up. Drink water, milk, fruit juice, and vegetable juice (which contain the mineral salts you lose when you sweat).

3. Get eight hours of sleep each night!

When you sleep, your cells renew themselves and your body regains the energy you have used during the day. Eight hours is a good amount of sleep to aim for. Here is some advice for a good night's sleep:

• Get up and go to bed at the same time each day.
• Don't eat too much in the evening.
• Don't watch too much TV (and avoid scary movies, which could give you nightmares).
• Before going to sleep, read a few pages of a good book!
• If you're having trouble falling asleep, drink a glass of hot milk (milk contains calcium, which helps you sleep).

Don't watch SCARY movies ...

... instead, read a good book!

4. Try these simple exercises!

• Squats:
Keep your legs together and stretch your arms out in front of you. Bend your legs as if you were about to sit down on a stool. Repeat.

• Jumping jacks:
Keep your legs together and your arms down at your sides. Jump up a little, spreading your legs and raising your arms. Repeat.

• Toe touches:
Standing with your legs apart, touch the tip of your left foot with your right hand. Switch and touch the tip of your right foot with your left hand. Repeat.

• Side bends:
Keep your legs apart and place your hands on your hips. Lean your body left, then move back to the centre. Lean your body right, then move back to the centre. Repeat.

5. Say no to cigarettes, alcohol and drugs!

Being an athlete also means saying no to cigarettes, alcohol, and drugs.

These things are bad for you! Make the right choices, the intelligent choices. Choose what is best for your body and mind! You'll be healthier and have more energy.

If someone offers you cigarettes, alcohol or drugs, talk about it with your parents, teachers or other adults who you trust. They care about you, and will always give you good advice!

6. When you're scared ... use your head!

Tip number one: If you are feeling nervous before a race, relax. Breathe in and out slowly until you feel calm, strong, and confident.

Tip number two: Before any competition, try to imagine that everything will go well. If you have a downhill skiing race, for example, imagine that you have a great race! All champions do this. And it works. Try it!

Tip number three: If you are still feeling afraid or nervous, remember that at the end of the day, it's only a game!

7. A fit mouse never stops!

Playing sports is good for the mind and the body!

The ancient Romans said: *Mens sana in corpore sano* (a sound mind in a sound body). Sports help release nervous energy and aggression, help you make new friends, help you be part of a team, make you feel more confident, and help you to realise your goals ... so they can also help you overcome any shyness you might have!

8. Be disciplined and keep trying!

Remember: it's better to exercise little and often, rather than exercise hard every once in a while.

9. Choose a sport that is right for you!

Choose a sport that you like, but ask for advice from your doctor, as well as someone who has more experience than you. Everybody is different: Some people are suited for swimming, others for tennis, basketball, karate, fencing, football or horse riding ...

WHAT'S YOUR FAVOURITE SPORT?

10. Respect your opponent!

Whatever sport you practise, remember to respect your opponent! A true champion knows how to win, but he or she also knows how to lose!

As the famouse French scholar Pierre de Coubertin said in 1896 when promoting the new Olympics: 'The important thing in the Olympic Games is not winning but taking part'.

All sports teach us to know ourselves better. They can even create good feelings between athletes of different nations and heritages!

TWO KARATE EXPERTS BOW TO EACH OTHER!

ABOUT THE AUTHOR

Born in New Mouse City, Mouse Island, GERONIMO STILTON is Rattus Emeritus of Mousomorphic Literature and of Neo-Ratonic Comparative Philosophy. For the past twenty years, he has been running The Rodent's Gazette, New Mouse City's most widely read daily newspaper.

Stilton was awarded the Ratitzer Prize for his scoops on *The Curse of the Cheese Pyramid* and *The Search for Sunken Treasure*. He has also received the Andersen Prize for Personality of the Year. His works have been published all over the globe.

In his spare time, Mr. Stilton collects antique cheese rinds and plays golf. But what he most enjoys is telling stories to his nephew Benjamin.

The Rodent's Gazette

1. Main entrance
2. Printing presses (where everything is printed)
3. Accounts department
4. Editorial room (where editors,
illustrators, and designers work)
5. Geronimo Stilton's office
6. Geronimo's botanical garden

MAP OF NEW MOUSE CITY

MAP OF MOUSE ISLAND

1. Big Ice Lake
2. Frozen Fur Peak
3. Slipperyslopes Glacier
4. Coldcreeps Peak
5. Ratzikistan
6. Transratania
7. Mount Vamp
8. Roastedrat Volcano
9. Brimstone Lake
10. Poopedcat Pass
11. Stinko Peak
12. Dark Forest
13. Vain Vampires Valley
14. Goosebumps Gorge
15. The Shadow Line Pass
16. Penny-Pincher Castle
17. Nature Reserve Park
18. Las Ratayas Marinas
19. Fossil Forest
20. Lake Lake
21. Lake Lakelake
22. Lake Lakelakelake
23. Cheddar Crag
24. Cannycat Castle
25. Valley of the Giant Sequoia
26. Cheddar Springs
27. Sulphurous Swamp
28. Old Reliable Geyser
29. Vole Vale
30. Ravingrat Ravine
31. Gnat Marshes
32. Munster Highlands
33. Mousehara Desert
34. Oasis of the Sweaty Camel
35. Cabbagehead Hill
36. Rattytrap Jungle
37. Rio Mosquito
38. Mousefort Beach
39. San Mouscisco
40. Swissville
41. Cheddarton
42. Mouseport
43. New Mouse City
44. Pirate Ship of Cats

HAVE YOU READ ALL OF GERONIMO'S ADVENTURES?

- ☐ *Lost Treasure of the Emerald Eye*
- ☐ *The Curse of the Cheese Pyramid*
- ☐ *Cat and Mouse in a Haunted House*
- ☐ *I'm Too Fond of My Fur!*
- ☐ *Four Mice Deep in the Jungle*
- ☐ *Paws Off, Cheddarface!*
- ☐ *Fangs and Feasts in Transratania*
- ☐ *Attack of the Pirate Cats*

HAPPY READING!